THE DIRTY COWBOY

BY

AMY TIMBERLAKE

PICTURES BY

ADAM REX

FARRAR STRAUS GIROUX
NEW YORK

At the end of two fence lines and right at the rock called The Praying Iguana lived a cowboy in a tin-roofed shack.

Every morning, he'd call his dog, mount his horse, and spend the day tracking stray longhorn cattle on the New Mexico range.

Every evening, he'd stoke his fire and fry up some bacon, beans, and potatoes while whistling "The Streets of Laredo."

Now, one morning—and no one knows for sure what drives a man to it—this cowboy decided to clean himself up. Regular bathers would've said the signs had been plenty clear: the cowboy's hair housed thirty-two fleas and a small gray spider.

On three recent occasions he'd discovered a tumbleweed in his chaps. A flurry of flies flocked round his body buzzing so persistently that he experienced a distinct loss of hearing in his left ear. And the cowboy's stench stuck to passersby like mud splashed up from a wagon wheel.

But whatever his reason, on that fateful day, the cowboy picked a doodlebug out of his right eyebrow and said,

This ol' boy needs a bath.

So the cowboy saddled his horse, packed up twenty-two strips of jerky, a canteen of water, and a nearly new bar of lye soap, and called for his dog. The dog opened one eye, sniffed at the air, and followed his friend's warm, familiar smell as though he was following a trail of T-bone steaks. Off they went.

A long, rambling ride later, the river came into view.

It was a sight for sore eyes! The river idled around red boulders, and afternoon sun spangled the water copper and gold. The cowboy tied his horse near water, grass, and a bit of shade. Then he removed his boots and spurs. He unfastened his neckerchief and pulled off his socks, vest, shirt, pants, and long johns, and heaped them at the dog's feet. Above the dog's head, he hung his hat on a spindly bush of screwbean mesquite.

Then, yelling

WWHOOOOOwheeEEE!

the cowboy ran—naked as a newborn pack rat—straight into the water.

He scrubbed his face, his nose, his eyebrows. He lathered his arms; he lathered his legs. He soaped under his knees, into his armpits, and over his belly. He buffed his toenails till they shone like little moons. He washed behind his ears, around his elbows, and across his Adam's apple. He sang songs about rivers flowin', cattle lowin', and cowboys crowin'. Water spurted between his teeth and slapped under his hands. Ahh!

When the river ran clear and his skin puckered up like a prickly pear, the cowboy declared his bath done. He shook himself off and went to get his clothes. Maybe his duds could use a little soaping, too.

Now, that old dog was guarding the cowboy's clothes just as he'd been told. And as the cowboy got closer, the dog sniffed the air, paused for a look, then sniffed again. He observed a lopsided lope and heard warbly singing—both characteristic of his cowboy. But still, the dog thought something wasn't right.

Where was that sweaty, wild boar–like smell that clung to the cowboy like a second pair of clothes? Where was the smell of black pepper and mesa mud? And where, oh where, was the smell of cow?

That settled it. If a cowboy doesn't smell like cow, it ain't a cowboy. So whoever was headed the dog's way wouldn't be touching those clothes.

"rrrrRRR," said the dog, baring both his teeth.

"C'mon, dawg," said the cowboy, chuckling. "Give me my duds."

"GGgggrRR!" said the dog, backing up till he was squatted atop the filthy heap.

The cowboy laughed again and reached for his pants, a corner of which stuck out from under the dog's paw.

The dog took a jump for the cowboy's arm.

The cowboy leaped back, tripped over a rock, somersaulted, and splashed into the river at the horse's feet.

"eeEEooouuuu," said the horse, rearing bug-eyed and tripping aside to watch both the cowboy and the dog warily.

"That's about as funny as a kick in the behind with a sharp-toed boot," the cowboy mumbled to himself.

Dawg!

said the cowboy, water running off
his chin, as he pulled himself out of
the river.

You git!

He pointed to a pile of rocks
far in the distance that looked
like a giant horned toad.

"rrr r r," said the dog, raising
his head.

"You heard me," said the
cowboy. "Git!"

"RRRrrrGGGh!" said the dog
for emphasis.

Nothing the cowboy said or did
could convince the dog of the
cowboy's identity. The dog refused
to budge from atop the clothes.

The cowboy picked up a stick
and threw it.

Fetch!

he said. The dog and the cowboy
watched the stick land with a thud
a good ten feet away.

The cowboy put his hands on
his hips and called the dog by his
full name. "Eustace Shackelford
Montana!" The dog turned around
on the pile of clothes and lay down.

The cowboy sang the dog's favorite ballad, "Biscuits, a Fire, and a Mexico Moon." The dog joined in with a howl during the chorus, but raised his hackles when the cowboy made a grab for the clothes.

Finally, when the cowboy noticed the lowering sun getting stuck in the tines of a saguaro cactus, he decided it was time for action. He'd wrestle that dog till the dog plain gave up. (Heck, the dog only had two teeth.)

Now, this is the
truth (and the horse
will testify): right
there and then,
that dog and
that cowboy
made the biggest
dust devil the West
ever saw. Wrestling-dirt
swirled into the sky,
forming a sticky
brown cloud.

But the dog and
the cowboy didn't notice.
The dog was up. The cowboy
was under. The dog wiggled sideways.
The cowboy finagled the otherways. Grime
got into everything. Dust stiffened the cowboy's
hair, crept between his eyelashes, and staked
a claim on his eyebrows. The dog's nose
turned muddy and his tongue slopped
in a wet grit that rivaled the muck
of a pigsty. Meanwhile, dirt
sullied the clear New
Mexico air.

The clothing didn't fare too well. All that tussling took its effect.

First, the stitching started to give, then the buttons popped,

and then thread on thread gave way with a ripping

sound like creaking before thunder.

Pretty soon, that dust devil filled with color: long-john red, neckerchief yellow, sock blue, and even fancy-vest purple. Why, it almost looked like a smudgy rainbow.

Finally, the cowboy and the dog found themselves squared off over the shirt. The dog had the back of the shirt. The cowboy had the right arm. And they were pulling each other in circles, tugging this way and that.

"CcccRRRRRRRRRrrrrEEEE iiiiiippP!"

The cowboy catapulted onto his behind.

"Shoot," said the cowboy. In his hand was the right arm of his shirt. The back of the shirt lay at the feet of his panting dog. Meanwhile, the saguaro cactus was now cradling the sun in the crook of one arm. So the cowboy walked over to his horse, pulled a piece of jerky out of his pack, and sat on a rock to gnaw things through.

Now, that dog had a chance to sniff again. And slowly the cowboy began to smell in perspective.

The dog smelled tumbleweed, prickly pear, and wet mud. When the cowboy wiped his brow, a wash of sweaty wild boar tickled the dog's nose.

And, finally, the cowboy sighed. The cowboy's breath smelled like black pepper and cow jerky! It was the dog's cowboy after all!

said the dog.

But it was too late for apologies. What was done was done. The
cowboy found his hat and his boots. But most all of his clothes
were best set aside for patchwork quilts, or for scrub jays making
their nests cozy. There wasn't much of anything for a grown
cowboy.

Not long afterward, the sticky dust-devil cloud cracked open
and rained. The cacti burst into bloom like firecrackers, and
suddenly the landscape was dotted with color and ribboned with
water.

The cowboy sighed and ruffled the dog's ears.

"Why, look at that, Eustace," he said. "Ain't that purty."

The dog looked up at the cowboy and licked his fingers.

The cowboy laughed.

"You sure are a sight," he said, plucking nettles out of the dog's
hide.

The story goes that the cowboy walked home—bare as a shorn sheep—from the river to his tin-roofed shack. He wore his boots and his hat, but otherwise he was naked as a nickel. The horse, skittish after all that wrangling, was led by his bridle. The dog trotted at the cowboy's side, hoping for jerky handouts.

The rain fell the whole way home. The rainwater was so grimy, the fresh soaking didn't clean off the wrestling-dirt at all. But as the cowboy looked up into that dust-devil sky, he had an idea. Next year's bath, he'd bring a bristle brush.

For Papa, who told the story,
and for Yi-Yi, who said it was true
—A.T.

For Mom and Dad, who paid for art lessons
—A.R.

Library of Congress Cataloging-in-Publication Data
Timberlake, Amy.
The dirty cowboy / Amy Timberlake ; pictures by Adam Rex.— 1st ed.
   p.   cm.
   Summary: Telling his faithful dog to make sure nobody touches his clothes but him, a
cowboy jumps into a New Mexico river for a bath, not realizing just how much the
scrubbing will change his scent.
   ISBN 0-374-31791-7
   [1. Cowboys—Fiction. 2. Baths—Fiction. 3. Dogs—Fiction. 4. New Mexico—
Fiction. 5. Tall tales. 6. Humorous stories.] I. Rex, Adam, ill. II. Title.

PZ7.T479 Di 2003
[Fic]—dc21

2001053224